The Boat Race

SCRIBBLERS

IT was a warm, sunny day. Little Bear and his friends were exploring the garden shed.

Bramwell Brown was tearing up sheets of old newspaper.

'What are you making?' asked Little Bear.

'Wait and see!' said Bramwell, as he folded a sheet of paper over and over again. At last he held it up for the others to see.

'IT'S a boat,' cried Little Bear. 'Please make more. We can race them down the stream.'

Bramwell had plenty of newspaper and soon he had made everyone a paper boat.

'Let's try one out in Sailor's bath,' suggested Rabbit. Sailor was having a lovely time rowing round and round an old tin bath.

'WE just want to see if this floats,' said Rabbit, lowering his paper boat into the water and giving it a push. It sailed well at first, but then they watched sadly as it went all soggy and fell over in the water.

'Oh no!' cried Little Bear. 'It's sinking.'

B RAMWELL examined the paper boat.

'Ah, that's because they're not really boats at all,' he said.
'They're hats - pirate hats!'

'We can't have a boat race with *hats*,' grumbled Duck.

'Of course we can,' said Bramwell. 'We'll build boats out
of things in the shed and wear the hats to sail them.'

'A boat *each*?' asked Little Bear.

'Well, let's make two boats,'
suggested Bramwell, 'and Sailor
can use his own, so that makes
three. That's enough for a race.'

THERE were lots of bits and pieces in the shed to make into boats. Rabbit found a little wooden basket. 'This could be our boat, Little Bear,' he said. 'We just need a mast and a sail.'

Sailor was helping Jolly, Duck and Bramwell build a raft out of sticks.

'WE'LL need to make it strong,' said Duck. 'I don't want to get wet feet.'

'We won't need a mast for our boat,' laughed Bramwell. 'Jolly has such a long neck, he can hold the sail!'

'WHAT sail?' asked Duck, looking around.

Bramwell found a green umbrella.

'If Jolly holds this,' he said, 'the wind will catch it and blow us along. We're sure to win the race.'

When all the boats were ready, the toys pulled them down to the stream. Sailor tied his boat to the raft and had a ride all the way there.

'This is easy sailing,' he laughed.

JUST as the boats touched the water, a big gust of wind blew them away from the bank. Sailor was still tied to the raft, so he went too.

'I can't win if I'm tied on the back!' he cried.

Rabbit didn't have time to jump into his boat.

'Stop!' he called to Little Bear, as he ran along the bank. 'Wait for me!'

But Little Bear couldn't stop.

'You're going too fast,' puffed Rabbit.

'Lower your sail and you'll slow down.'

Little Bear climbed the mast and tried to untie the sail.

He didn't see the bridge over the stream.

'Look out!' cried Rabbit, but it was too late.

Duck's raft had nearly caught up with Little Bear's boat when the mast hit the bridge. Little Bear flew through the air, bounced off Jolly's umbrella and landed in Bramwell's paws.

'Phew! That was lucky,' gasped Little Bear.

'Not for us,' grumbled Duck. 'Our raft was only meant for three. And now there are four of us. You are making us sink.'

It was true; they floated under the bridge, but the raft was getting lower and lower in the water.

'HELP!' they all shouted together.

'Where's Rabbit?' cried Duck. 'He was there on the bank a moment ago.'

THEN they heard a familiar noise. Looking up, they saw the little wooden plane, with Rabbit as pilot, flying across the garden - Rabbit to the rescue!

'Catch this rope!' he called to the sinking sailors. 'I'll give you a tow.'

Bramwell caught the rope and tied it to the raft. As Rabbit towed them to the bank, Sailor untied his boat and sailed on down the stream.

Rabbit landed the plane and bounced over to where the others were waiting.

'Oh, thank you, Rabbit!' cried Little Bear. 'You saved us all, just in time!'

'It's a pity nobody won the race, though,' muttered Duck.

But at that moment Sailor came rowing his boat back up the stream.

'I T looks as though *I* won the race,' he laughed. 'I'm the only one left with a boat!'

'Well done, Sailor,' said Jolly. 'In future I think we will leave all the sailing to you. We'll just stay on dry land and watch!'

Little Bear's Dragon

OLD Bear was reading a story to Little Bear. It was an exciting story about a dragon who lived in a secret cave.

'Are there any real dragons?' asked Little Bear, as he hid under his blanket.

'I haven't seen one,' said Old Bear. 'But we could make you a dragon mask if you like. Then you could pretend to be a real dragon.'

'And I could live in a cave,' squeaked Little Bear, 'and make scary dragon noises!'

'That would surprise the other toys,' laughed Old Bear.

Old Bear found a little box and cut it in half.

'This will be your dragon head,' he told Little Bear. 'Look, its mouth opens and shuts.'

'Will it breathe fire?' asked Little Bear.

'I don't think I can manage *that*,' laughed Old Bear.

LITTLE Bear
had found an old
tablecloth. He draped
it over a chair.

'I've made a cave!'
he cried. 'It's all dark
inside. A dragon
could easily
hide in there.'

OLD Bear had nearly finished the dragon head. He painted it green with fiery orange eyes.

'It needs some sharp teeth to look really scary,' said Little Bear. 'I'll make it some.'

O N a piece of paper he drew a long row of pointy
teeth - up and down, up and down. Then he cut them out.
Old Bear stuck them in the dragon's mouth and added a
piece of ribbon to make a long, forked tongue.

  '*Now* it looks scary!' gasped Little Bear, taking a step
back.

  Old Bear lifted the dragon mask and slipped it over Little
Bear's head.

  'Grrr,' said Little Bear, as loud as he could.

  'You look like a very fierce dragon now,' said Old Bear.
'I'll just go and find you a tail.'

LITTLE Bear hurried to his cave to practise his roars. First he did little roars like a baby dragon. Then he tried louder ones to sound more fierce, and finally really big ones:

'Grrrrrr!'

The roaring made him feel quite tired, so he decided to see if there was room for a small dragon to lie down in his cave. In no time at all Little Bear had settled down in a corner and fallen fast asleep.

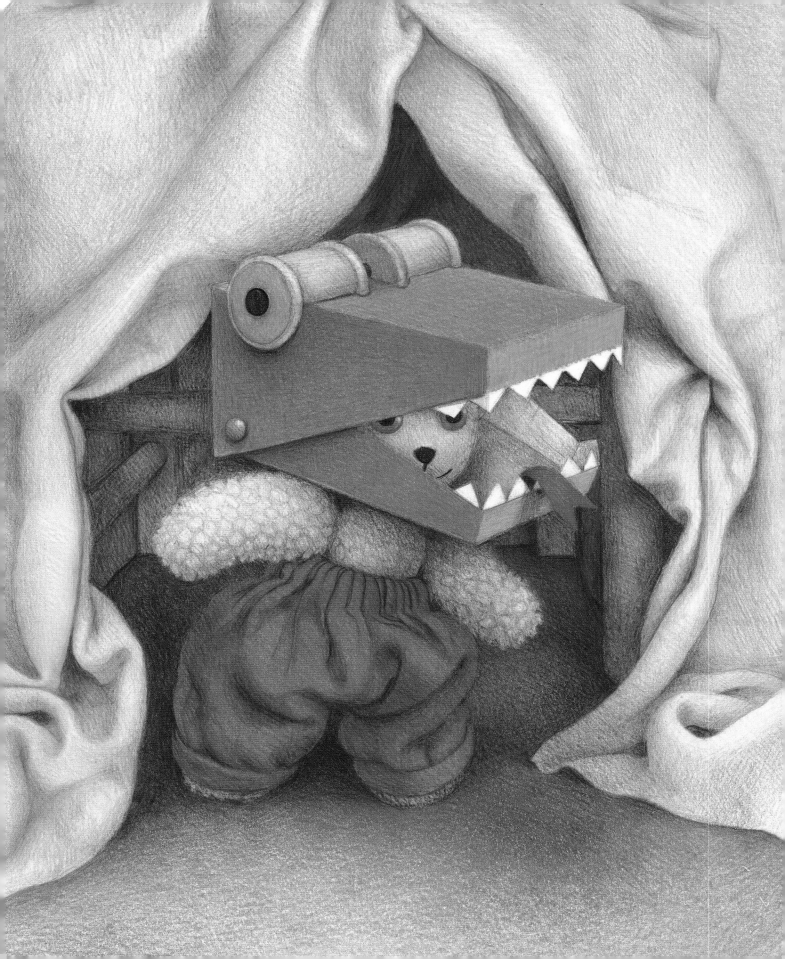

HE was still sleeping when Jolly Tall and Rabbit arrived.

'Can you hear a sort of breathing noise?' asked Rabbit, gazing around the room.

'It's coming from in here,' said Jolly, peering into the tablecloth cave. Rabbit looked in too, then jumped in surprise. 'HELP!' he cried. 'It's a dragon. Quick! Run!'

Jolly galloped towards the door and bumped into Sailor.

'RUN!' shouted Jolly, 'There's a dragon in there.'

'Is it breathing fire?' asked Sailor, nervously.

'Not right now,' said Rabbit. 'But I'm sure it might do at any moment.'

'I'll get some water to put its fire out,' said Sailor, 'just in case.'

'Good idea. Dragons are probably frightened of water,' said Rabbit.

'What else are they frightened of?' asked Jolly.

'Only other dragons, probably,' said Rabbit. 'Bigger ones!'

'Perhaps we could pretend to be a bigger dragon?' suggested Jolly. 'Then the small dragon would see the big one and it would stay in its cave.'

'And not breathe fire on us!' cried Rabbit.

Jolly and Rabbit hurried away to make a dragon costume. Sailor returned to bravely guard the cave.

HE was still sitting there
when Old Bear called to him.
'Have you seen Little Bear?'
he asked, 'Or is he still in
the cave?'

BEFORE Sailor could reply, there was a huge roar and into the room marched a big green dragon, with a long yellow neck.

Sailor nearly threw his buckets of water over it, but then he saw its feet and realised just in time that it was only Jolly and Rabbit in their dragon costume.

'Quick!' he called. 'Old Bear says Little Bear is in the cave. The dragon must have captured him.'

'We'll save him!' cried Jolly.

Before Old Bear could explain, Sailor joined the others in the dragon suit and the eight-legged monster rushed towards the cave, roaring and stamping its feet.

'WHAT'S all the noise?' cried the Little Bear dragon, as it staggered sleepily out of the tablecloth cave. He saw the fierce, big dragon.

'HELP!' cried the little dragon, as it dashed back inside the cave.

'It worked!' shouted Rabbit. 'The little dragon was scared of us and we've frightened it away.'

'But we're too late,' sniffed Jolly. 'It must have eaten Little Bear; it was wearing his trousers!'

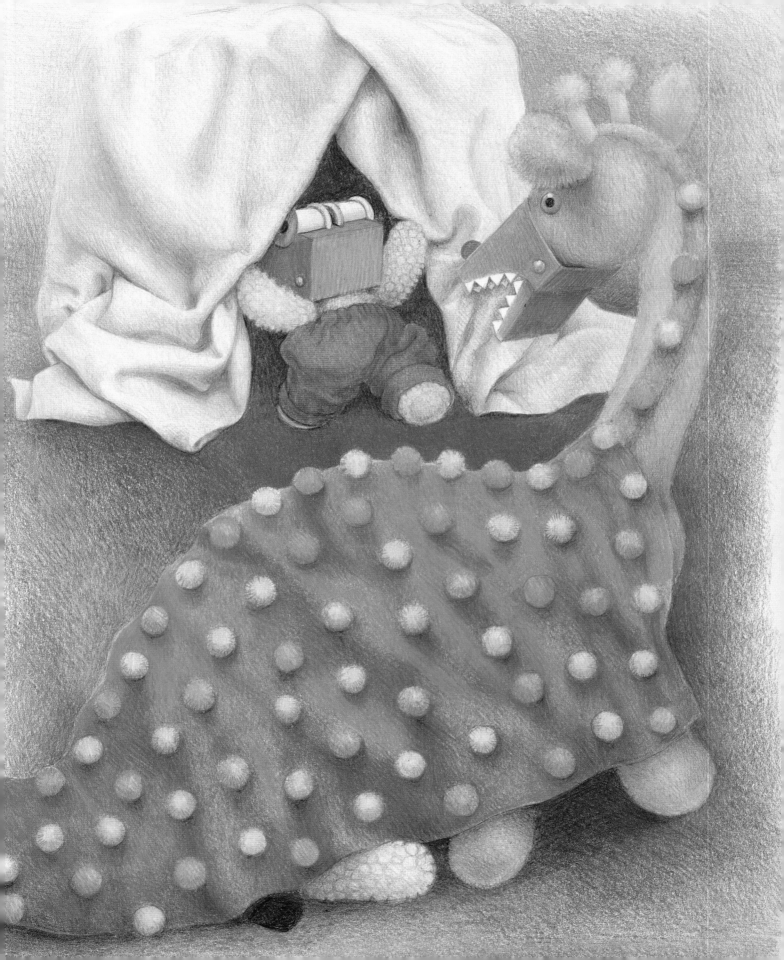

OLD Bear hurried over.
'Don't worry,' he laughed.
'I think I might have a surprise
for you.'
He stood by the entrance to the
cave and called, 'Come out, little
dragon.'
And out it came...very slowly.
Old Bear carefully lifted off
the little dragon's cardboard head.
And there was Little Bear
looking a bit nervous, but all in
one piece.
The others cheered. Old Bear picked
up Little Bear and carried him over
to the big dragon.

'DON'T worry,' he said. 'This isn't a real dragon either. Jolly, Rabbit and Sailor are in there.'

'Are they?!' gasped Little Bear. 'Did they think I was a real dragon, too?'

'They did,' laughed Old Bear, 'and they were trying to frighten you away. Now, after all that excitement, I think it's bedtime for all dragons.'

'Then will you read us another story?' asked Little Bear. 'About something not *quite* so scary this time.'

For Nigel, Gill, Sam and Sarah

SALARIYA

www.salariya.com

This edition published in Great Britain in MMXV by Scribblers, a division of Book House,
an imprint of The Salariya Book Company Ltd
25 Marlborough Place,
Brighton BN1 1UB

www.scribblersbooks.com
www.janehissey.co.uk

First published in Great Britain in MCMXCIX by Hutchinson Children's Books

ISBN-13: 978-1-908973-69-6

1 3 5 7 9 8 6 4 2

A CIP catalogue record for this book is available from the British Library.

Printed and bound in China.
Printed on paper from sustainable sources.